LITTLE JOHNNY SUPERMAN AND HIS D-DAY ADVENTURE

A TRUE TALE FOR YOUNG AND OLD

By

Francoise Johnson

Illustrations By
ABC Educational Materials & Training

Age 8 and up

ISBN: 9798555419583 (paperback)

Johnny was a little boy who lived in a house, in a small town, in the United States, with his parents and his brother and sister. His dad owned a grocery store, his mom stayed home to raise the children, and Johnny's grandpa, who lived nearby, owned several large corn fields.

Most of all, what Johnny loved to do was to read comic books about Superman. He read so many he wanted to be Superman.

If I were Superman, he thought, I could help my grandpa in his corn fields: In just one sweep, zoom, I could cut the stalks, remove the cobs and store them in the tall silo on his farm. In just one sweep, I could unload the boxes of canned goods from my dad's truck, empty them and place them on the store shelves. In just one sweep I would clean all the windows in the house for my mom.

It could be so wonderful to fly all over the place like Superman and do good deeds. Johnny dreamed to be him.

Meanwhile, on another land in Europe far, far away, something terrible was happening: A little man, with a short mustache under his nose, with arrows coming out of his eyes and bombs in his mouth was slowly turning into a monster. He was destroying everything around him. He bombed many countries: Hungary, Lithuania, Poland, Belgium, England, France…Many people were dying, the rest was very scared.

On top of it, this tyrant was creating thousands of small ones like him. They were moving into people's homes, taking their food, their money, the ladies' jewelries, and the children's toys. It was awful. Everywhere there was devastation and pain. Children were terrified.

Back in the United States, where Johnny lived, an important Army general learned what was happening in Europe. He could not believe it! He was concerned...What if, he thought, all these monsters over there grew wings and flew over here to destroy everything? Something needs to be done. We, Americans, need to stop these creatures. He talked to the President and to his friends. Everyone agreed we had to go to Europe and get rid of these beasts before they came over here.

Johnny heard the General's call for all the good men to go with him to stop these dragons. Johnny was only sixteen (16) years old at the time, but he did not hesitate. He claimed he was eighteen (18), enlisted in the army, went to New York where he jumped into a big ship.

There, he crossed the entire Atlantic Ocean from one side all the way to the other.

When he arrived at the edge of the European continent, on a beach in Normandy, he jumped out the boat and ran amidst the creatures' bullets trying to hit him…He ran and fought nonstop for an entire year, avoiding the blows, getting rid of the beasts all around him.

After an entire year: VICTORY! No more monsters, they were all dead! Gone!

People in Europe were so happy they were embracing Johnny and his friends. Everybody was dancing and singing in the street!

Here, at home, in the United States, people were happy too. The town organized a big parade. When Johnny came home, everybody wanted to hug him. He was a hero and his parents were very proud of him.

Today, Johnny is alive and well. He is now ninety-four (94) years old. He is a grandpa. The day Johnny arrived on the beach in Normandy was so important that, all over the world, people decided to call it the "D-DAY," and to celebrate it every year on June 6.

On D-Day, last year, a European newspaperman interviewed him on television: “Johnny,” asked the journalist, “you were on the Normandy beach.” “What did you do? how did you feel? What was it like?” Johnny looked at this man and with a big laughter and great humility, he answered:” You know, I thought I was Superman, I just did what I had to do.”

“But, The journalist said: “Johnny, you were Superman, you still are Superman! It’s because of you and guys like you that Europe is now a free continent! It’s because of you and guys like you, that my country, France, is a free country! And it’s because of you and guys like you that I am a free European French citizen! I thank you Johnny from the bottom of my heart.” And he gave him a big hug.

D-DAY? DO YOU WANT TO KNOW MORE ABOUT IT?

Remember that it happens every year, in the month of June, on the 6th! So, when June comes around next year, pay attention, at the beginning of the month, tell your parents that you want to watch the D-Day celebrations on television on June 6th. Most stations carry it. Your parents may ask you why. Just explain to them that you have read the true story of Little Johnny Superman and his D-Day Adventure, and that you like to know more about this historic event. Most parents will be happy to help you with your research. A few parents may object if they think you are too young. In this case, just ask them again the following year.

On television, you will see the President of the United States, the President of Europe, the President of France, many Army Generals, and many people honoring all American heroes who, just like Little Johnny Superman, fought the monsters of that time, but passed away. Little Johnny Superman was a lucky man who came out of his adventure alive, but many heroes like him, were not lucky. Also, again with your parents' permission, you can go on Google, on your phone or your tablet, and google "D-Day." You will be able to read all about it. You will be amazed to learn about this great American victory.

EUROPE

Europe is a continent just like America is a continent. A continent is much larger than a country. A continent is composed of many countries.
FRANCE, BELGIUM, POLAND, LITHUANIA, HUNGARY, ENGLAND ARE COUNTRIES. DO YOU WANT TO KNOW WHERE ARE ALL THESE COUNTRIES IN EUROPE?

Take a map of the world, or a globe showing planet Earth. Find America. Find the United States where Little Johnny Superman Lived. Next to the United States, on each side, you see a lot of blue, which means there is a huge amount of water there. These are oceans. On the west side you see the Pacific Ocean. Way, on the other side is the Atlantic Ocean. This is the ocean that Little Johnny crossed in his ship, from part to part. On the other side of it, straight across the United States is a huge mass of land called Europe. This is where he landed, in a small country there called France, and on one of the beaches in Normandy, which is a region in France. Try to find it on your map or on your globe.

Belgium is next to and on the other side of France on the map, and north of it. It is a small, lovely area. Next to Belgium, you find Germany and north of it, you will find Poland, another great European country. Lithuania is near Poland, north of it. It is an interesting and beautiful place. Inland, south of Poland, is Hungary. A nice country. England is an island, detached but near the European continent. It is north of France. It is also called the United Kingdom.

If you do not have a map of the world or a globe, go to Google, on your phone or your tablet, and look up these countries. You will find your discoveries remarkably interesting. Our planet Earth is made of many beautiful countries, filled with wonderful people. Let us be kind to each other and take care of our planet.

YOUR FAMILY'S SUPERHEROES? DO YOU KNOW WHO THEY ARE?

Do you know your parents' and your grandparents' personal story? Have you talked to them about D-Day? Did someone in your family contribute to this heroic event? If so, what are they saying to you?

Little Johnny was not the only remarkable young man participating in the D-DAY adventure? Hundreds of American ships, thousands of Americans went with him. It was a long time ago so most of them are no longer alive, but their story and their memory still live in the hearts of their families.
Perhaps, when you ask, you will find out that, although none of your ancestors joined in D-Day, other important events affected some of your family members. Many parents, for example, worked long hours to provide for their children. Many parents are Heroes. Sometimes it is a big brother or a sister. Or an uncle or an aunt. Grand parents are well known for their devotion to their grandchildren. In these times of Corona Virus pandemic, we see essential workers, risking their lives in hospitals to save people. Everyday we salute all, among us, who fight to stop this dangerous disease. They are our National Heroes!

Do you know who are the superheroes in your family? Take the time to research them. I am sure that you will find them. What did they say to you? Do you admire them? What are their qualities? Can you describe them or write about them or draw them for me? If you do this, email me the story of your superhero. I love to know about it. My e-mail address is in your book. I will respond to your story.

D-DAY SONGS

D- Day has inspired many artists of all kinds and of all nationalities: singers, musicians, cineastes, photographs, poets, writers, just to name a few.

We can still hear the music and the songs created to celebrate DDay. Such great American singers as Jim Radford, Shirlie Holliman, Nat King Cole, and many others have memorialized it. We are fortunate that new technologies have enabled us today to listen to them.

The best and easiest way, if you want to hear these songs, is to google "D-Day songs" on your computer or your tablet and, with your parents' permission, to listen to them. You can, of course, purchase some of these albums.

Questions? Feedback?

Write to Little Johnny at the following email address.
francoisejohnson@sbcglobal.net
Subject: Little Johnny.
He is looking forward to hearing from you, and he will answer you.

Made in the USA
Monee, IL
08 January 2021

56935044R00017